The Setting

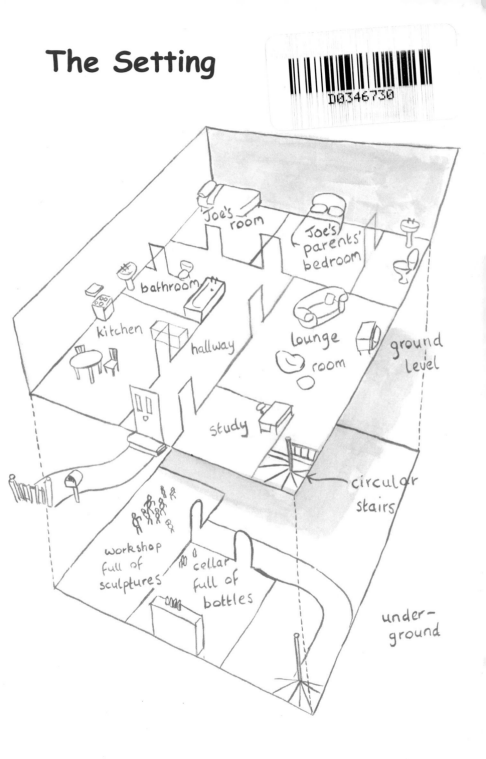

CONTENTS

CHAPTER 1

Joe's Secret Tunnel

"Do you want to see under my house?" said Joe to his new friend.

"Yes," said Peter, "but why?"

"Everyone wants to see under my house. It's really spooky. You don't have to go outside first. You just go down the circular stairs. You walk down to the bottom and there's this tunnel and …"

"Let's go then," said Peter.

"Er … we can't go yet," said Joe.

"Why not?"

"We'll just wait till Mum goes out. She's going across the road to see Mrs Philpott," Joe said in a whisper.

"Why do we have to wait?" asked Peter.

"I'm not allowed to go down there any more," said Joe quietly.

"Why aren't you?" Peter asked.

"You know how I want to be rich when I grow up?" said Joe.

"Yes."

"Well, I was making my friends pay fifty pence to go under the house. Only fifty pence. That's not much."

Joe went on. "Mum says I'm not to do it any more. She doesn't care that she is keeping me poor. She doesn't care at all about that."

"Are you going to make me pay?" asked Peter.

"I told you, I'm not allowed," Joe said with a frown.

"Good," said Peter.

Then Joe smiled, "You can make a donation. You know how people make donations to good causes. My future is a good cause."

Joe's Mum called, "Joe, I'm just going across the road to see Mrs Philpott."

"Bye Mum," said Joe.

The Dark Tunnel

The door slammed.

"Now!" said Joe.
They went out of the kitchen and across the hall. There was the circular stairway. Down, down, down they both went.

At the bottom of the stairs was the tunnel. The light was dim at first but soon it became pitch black. Peter sucked in his breath. He'd always been a bit scared of the dark.

"Don't put your hands on the walls," Joe said, "you might get bitten."

"Nothing lives down here," Peter said, his voice shaking a little. "It's too dark."

"What about spiders? They live in the dark," said Joe.

Peter took his hands off the wall. Quickly.

The narrow tunnel went round a corner. Peter's head scraped along some bricks.

"I don't know where I'm going. I need to touch the walls," said Peter.

"Just follow me," said Joe. "I know the way. Listen to my feet. Use your ears."

Then something trailed across Peter's face. "Hey stop!" he screamed. "Something is on me."

"Cobwebs," said Joe. "Don't worry about them."

Peter pulled at them. He tried to get them off but they were sticky.

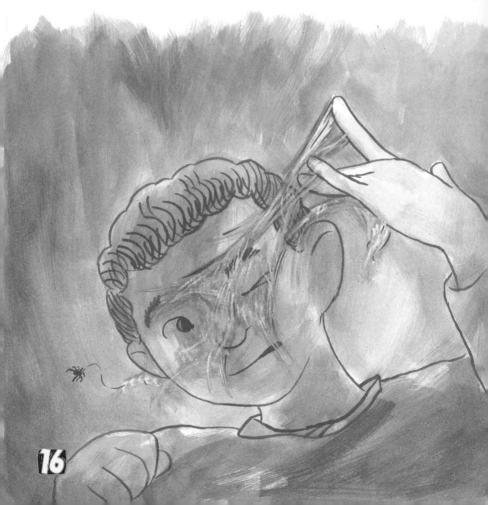

"Look," said Joe. "Light!"
"Watch your step here," he added.

It was too late. Peter was stepping
onto empty bottles. They were rolling
under his feet and he rolled with
them. He landed in the dirt on his
hands and knees.

Spiders or no spiders, Peter was going to hold onto the walls now.

As they walked past an opening to a room, Joe said, "We'd better hurry past here."

Peter tried to hurry. He wanted to ask
"Why?" but he was out of breath.

"Bang!" There was a loud explosion.
Glass splintered against the brick walls.
Peter thought he'd been shot.

"See what I mean?" said Joe.

"What was it?" Peter said, trying to sound calm.

"A ginger beer bottle. Dad makes his own ginger beer. Then he puts them down here. A bottle sometimes explodes if it is too gassy."

Now the tunnel opened out into a
large room. The room was dimly lit.
Peter saw a man in the corner. His
heart leapt in shock. His throat
closed. He couldn't speak.

Peter stood still. Then he started to see more people. They were all around him. The room was full of people.

CHAPTER 3

Who Are These People?

All the people stood very still. Their stillness was scary. There was something strange about them.

"These are Dad's sculptures," said Joe. "He used to be a sculptor but he had to give it up."

Suddenly the room was full of light and Joe was laughing.

"There are lights all the way," Joe
said, "but I think it's more fun
coming in the dark, don't you? Were
you scared?" he asked.

Peter stared at the sculptures. His heart was still in his throat and his hands were all wet. He tried to smile.

They heard footsteps above them.

"Oh-oh!" said Joe. "Mum's back. Now I'm in trouble."
He started walking back along the tunnel.

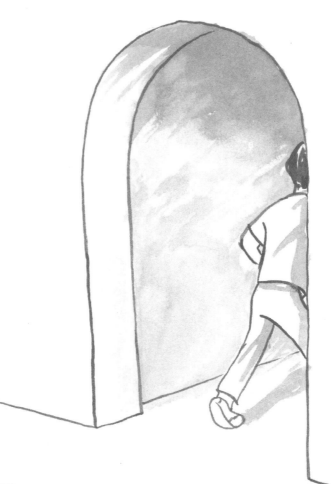

"I'll put the lights on now. Can you be very quiet so she doesn't know we're down here? OK? We'll try to sneak up the stairs without her knowing," Joe whispered.

Peter nodded his head.

Heavy Footsteps

They went slowly and carefully. Heavy footsteps thumped above them.

Peter whispered, "Does your mum wear heavy boots?"

"No, why?" asked Joe.

"Listen to her feet."

"You're right!" said Joe. He stopped walking. "That's not Mum!"

"Is it your dad?" asked Peter.

"Dad won't be home for ages," Joe said. "It must be a burglar. Listen to him."

They both listened. The feet were moving from one end of the house to the other.

"He'll wreck the place," Joe whispered.
"That's Mum's bedroom he's in now.
He must be stealing all her jewellery."

"Has your mum got a lot of jewellery?" asked Peter.

"Not much, no. Now she'll have nothing."

"What are we going to do?" asked
Peter. "We could ring the police."
His heart had started thumping again.
He was really scared now.

"That's it Peter. Good idea. We'll sneak into the kitchen and ring the police."

They could still hear the footsteps overhead.

"We'll wait until he goes to the other end of the house," said Joe.

"OK."

The noise of the footsteps faded.
They crept up the stairs.

They darted across the hall and into the kitchen. The telephone was in the corner.

Joe lifted the telephone. Then, with
a shock, they heard Joe's Mum.
"I'm home, Joe!" she called.
Before they could speak she walked
through the house towards her bedroom.

"Quick, stop her!" cried Peter, grabbing Joe's arm. "The burglar will get her."

"He'll probably hide when he hears her coming," said Joe.

CHAPTER

Saving Joe's Mum

"What if he doesn't? What if he kills her?" Peter was shaking like a leaf. "Do something," he hissed at Joe.

"If you knew Mum like I know Mum, you wouldn't worry," said Joe. "My mum's a match for any burglar."

"You're a coward!" said Peter in Joe's ear. "You don't care if your own mother gets killed."

There was the sound of a man's voice.

"Well, if you won't go I will!" Peter said. He raced along the hall to the bedroom. The burglar and Joe's Mum were near the double bed.

Peter leapt. He used all his force to land on the man's back.
"Leave her alone!" Peter shouted.

"What the …?" the man said, swinging
around and sending Peter spinning
onto the carpet.

"It's all right, Peter," said Joe's mum.
"This is Joe's dad. He's not hurting
me. We were just having a hug.

Peter jumped up and stood looking at them. Then he turned and ran out of the room.

"You knew it was your dad all the time, didn't you?" he snarled at Joe.

"I'm going to be a film maker when I grow up," said Joe. "I like to make scary things happen."

"I'm going home," said Peter.

"To make films you have to do things like that so you can see how people behave," said Joe.

Peter headed towards the door.

"I might be a writer as well," said Joe. "A writer can make all sorts of exciting things happen."

Peter stopped. Then he came back.

"Hey, why don't you make someone come down from outer space?" said Peter. "That's better than an old burglar."

"No, I'd rather have things coming up out of the ground. Monsters and things," said Joe. "You know, heaving up out of the ground."

"Wait! I've got a great idea!" cried
Peter. "What about a mad doctor?
Every time you go to the doctor, he
takes some part of you out. First it's
an eye or a kidney. Then it's your
tongue or something and he won't give
it back!"

"No! No way! That's too scary," said Joe. "That scares me to death."

GLOSSARY

 **allowed**
when you have permission

burglar
a thief who breaks
in to steal things

 circular
going around in a circle

 **donation**
to give money to
help someone else

explosion
a huge blow-up with
lots of noise

heaving
lifting up with
a great effort

pitch black
very, very, very dark

sculpture
solid artistic shapes
made by carving

sculptor
someone who carves
the shapes

splintered
break into very thin,
sharp pieces

Elizabeth Best

What is your favourite breakfast?

Oats and soya milk.

Who is your favourite cartoon character?

Felix the Cat.

What was your least favourite activity at school?

Homework.

Why is the sky blue?

Because they ran out of pink.

Paul Harrison

What is your favourite breakfast?

A steaming bowl of porridge when I feel like spoiling myself.

Who is your favourite cartoon character?

Calvin. He always finds the trapdoor to his imagination.

What was your least favourite activity at school?

Exams obviously. They are nothing short of torture.

Why is the sky blue?

So it is always easy to recognise.